Cacao Pods

Cacao pods can grow up to 30 centimetres in length, and weigh around 500 grams.

Harvest the Pods

The cacao pods ripen throughout the year, so cacao farmers harvest them every two to three weeks.

Fresh Cacao Beans

Each cacao pod contains between 20 and 60 seeds, or beans. The beans are surrounded by a white pulp. After the pod has been picked, the beans and pulp are scooped out. They are left to dry, and then the pulp is removed from the beans.

Dried Cacao Beans

The cacao beans are spread out to dry in the sun for about two weeks. Once dry, the beans turn from purple to dark brown. Then they are sorted. Only good-quality beans are put into sacks and sent to chocolate makers.

2 A WORLD of Chocolate

For thousands of years, people in Central and South America have ground up cacao beans to make drinks. Mayan Indians also used cacao beans as money, trading them for goods.

European Explorers Try Cacao Beans

More than 500 years ago, the explorer Christopher Columbus (1451–1506) made several journeys to the Caribbean and Central America. When he returned to Spain, Columbus brought cacao beans back for the Spanish king and queen to try. But most people didn't like the cacao drinks at first.

Mayan Indians Today
Many Mexicans today have Mayan ancestors. They keep their traditions alive by wearing Mayan costumes and performing Mayan dances on special occasions.

Chocolate CELEBRATIONS

Written by Sharon Parsons

Read how chocolate is helping to save me!

The la
shoul
from
only
telep
are
for

"Chocolate is a special treat we use to celebrate all kinds of events. We eat it and we drink it and we dip strawberries in it, too! If you look hard enough, you can even find dragons, like me, made of chocolate!"

Grusilda xxx

WWW.THELITERACYTOWER.COM

1 CHOCOLATE
Comes from Trees

Do you love the taste of chocolate?

Chocolate is a special treat that is used to celebrate all kinds of special occasions. Whether we're celebrating with a chocolate birthday cake, chocolate treats or a chocolate fountain, all that delicious chocolate starts out growing on a tree.

The Cacao Tree

The chocolate we eat is made from many ingredients. But all chocolate uses seeds taken from cacao pods, a fruit that grows on a cacao tree.

Cacao pods ripening on a cacao tree.

Cacao trees are usually grown on small family farms. The trees grow best in warm, humid places such as West Africa, Central America, Indonesia and Papua New Guinea.

Adding Flavour

As more and more people around the world tried the new cacao drink, they added flavourings such as sugar, honey, milk and vanilla, which made it taste better. For more than 250 years after it was discovered, people only used cacao as a drink.

When the World Discovered Chocolate

1600s
Europe

1500s
Spain

The Caribbean

Central America

South America

Chocolate Spreads

In the 1500s, chocolate drinks became popular in Spain. By the 1600s, other European countries were enjoying the drink, too. But it wasn't until the 1800s that chocolate makers in Europe worked out how to make "solid" chocolate for people to eat.

3 HOT CHOCOLATE
Drinks

In early times, people who lived in Central and South America made and drank hot chocolate. It was known as "xocolatl".

Xocolatl

People made the chocolate drink by grinding roasted cacao beans into a paste and mixing it with water. Then they created a frothy mixture by pouring it back and forth between two bowls or jugs.

Flavoursome ingredients such as cornmeal, chillies and spices were often added to the drink, too.

Adding chillies (right) made xocolatl very tasty.

Mayan Buildings

The Mayans were not only good at making hot chocolate — they also built large cities and pyramid-shaped temples. The Kukulkán Temple, built more than a thousand years ago, is one of the most visited Mayan buildings in Mexico.

A Modern Mexican Hot Chocolate Recipe
(Ask an adult to help you make this drink.)

Put in a large pot and whisk together:

- 2 cups of full cream milk
- 1 tablespoon of sugar or honey
- 1 teaspoon of vanilla essence or extract
- a pinch of salt
- a pinch of cinnamon

Add about 80 grams of chocolate pieces to the pot (cooking chocolate is best). Slowly heat and stir until the chocolate has melted.

Use a whisk to make the mixture frothy.

Pour into two mugs. Add one or two marshmallows to each mug.

¡Buen provecho!

(In Spanish, that means "Enjoy!")

Hot Chocolate Today
Today, hot chocolate is enjoyed around the world — but people have changed the early recipe to include other ingredients such as milk and marshmallows.

4 CHOCOLATE
on Special Days

Chocolates are special treats we enjoy when celebrating special days. Different chocolates and chocolate-flavoured foods are like symbols that we instantly recognise. Here are some of them

Valentine's Day

14 February
(Worldwide)

World Chocolate Day

7 July
(Worldwide)

Easter

March or April
(Worldwide)

Mother's Day

Happy Mother's Day!

May (AUS/NZ)
March (UK)

Chocolates make great gifts, because they're delicious and they often come in nice tins or boxes, too.

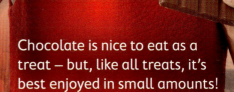

NO! THIS IS TOO MUCH TO EAT AT ONCE!

Chocolate is nice to eat as a treat — but, like all treats, it's best enjoyed in small amounts!

Christmas

25 December
(Worldwide)

Father's Day

HAPPY FATHER'S DAY

I ♥ DAD

September (AUS/NZ)
June (UK)

Birthdays

Whenever!
(Worldwide)

9

5 CHOCOLATE
Fountains

Over time people have used science and technology to help them create many kinds of chocolate treats. Chocolate fountains are a good example of how science, technology and delicious chocolate can mix!

Chocolate Flows

Chocolate fountains are a popular way to enjoy dessert at many big celebrations. But how does the chocolate keep flowing smoothly for so long?

Fountain Facts

Chocolate fountains were invented in Canada in 1991. Most restaurant fountains are about one metre high, and have about 15 kilograms of chocolate in them.

The world's tallest chocolate fountain is in Las Vegas, USA. It is eight metres tall. Almost two tonnes of chocolate can flow through it!

Flows Like a Chocolate Waterfall

Top tier

SCIENCE
Heat Melts Chocolate
Heat melts hard blocks or pieces of chocolate to form a smooth mixture. Chocolate is often melted before it is put into a chocolate fountain's bowl.

HEAT

SCIENCE and TECHNOLOGY
Heat Keeps Chocolate Warm
Melted chocolate is poured into a bowl in the base unit of the chocolate fountain. The base unit has a heater to keep the chocolate warm. Warm melted chocolate is able to flow through the fountain.

SCIENCE and TECHNOLOGY
Motor Makes Chocolate Flow
The fountain's base unit has a motor that turns a spiral drive. The spiral drive draws the warm chocolate upwards to the top tier. From there, the chocolate flows back down into the bowl. There, it combines with warmed chocolate before it goes back up to the top tier again.

Spiral drive

Bowl

Heater

Motor

Why Does Chocolate Harden Around a Strawberry?
As soon as the chocolate coats a cool or cold strawberry, the fruit's cooler temperature causes the chocolate to harden. Other favourite foods for dipping into melted chocolate are marshmallows, fruit and tiny biscuits.

6 A HUNDRED YEARS
of Chocolate

One family business that has been making delicious chocolates for more than 100 years is Haigh's Chocolates in Adelaide, Australia.

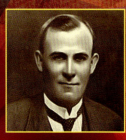

Alfred Haigh (1877–1933)

In 1915, Alfred Haigh began making and selling chocolates from a shop in Adelaide. By the 1930s, Haigh's chocolates were so popular he opened more shops.

Workers at Haigh's Chocolates in 1928

In 1933, Alfred's son Claude began running the business. His grandson John learnt how to make fine chocolates in Switzerland, and led the business from 1959. Alfred's great-grandsons, Alister and Simon, have been managing Haigh's since 1990.

(left to right) Simon, John & Alister Haigh run the business today.

Haigh's now has stores in South Australia, New South Wales, Victoria, and online, too.

How Haigh's Make Fine Chocolate

1. Buy Cocoa Beans
Haigh's buy cocoa beans from farmers for a fair price. Most are sustainably grown beans from farmers in places such as Peru, South America.

2. Cocoa Beans Roasted
Big batches of cocoa beans are roasted in large kettle roasters to take moisture out of the beans.

3. Shells Removed
A winnower machine removes the cocoa bean shells to reveal the cocoa nibs.

4. Grind Cocoa Nibs
A nib mill heats and grinds the cocoa nibs to make a liquid cocoa mass.

5. Mix Ingredients
A machine mixes ingredients such as the cocoa nibs, cocoa butter, vanilla and icing sugar to make a cocoa paste. (Milk powder is added for milk chocolate.)

6. Refine the Cocoa Paste
A refiner machine rolls the paste and changes it into fine cocoa powder.

7. Conche Cocoa Powder and Butter
A conching machine heats and mixes cocoa powder and cocoa butter to make smooth liquid chocolate.

8. Confectioners Make Chocolates
Confectioners are skilled people who turn the liquid chocolate into all kinds of amazing chocolates.

Pay Fair Prices
Haigh's pay fair prices to cacao bean farmers. That means the farmers can make enough money to live.

Winnowing

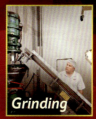
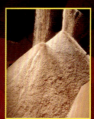

Grinding

Conching

Chocolate!

7 CHOCOLATE EASTER
Animals

In many countries around the world, chocolate bunnies are a symbol of Easter. That's because, in northern hemisphere countries such as the UK and the USA, Easter is in spring. Spring is when most baby rabbits are born.

In some countries, such as Australia, rabbits are a pest. So Australian chocolate-makers, such as Haigh's, decided that native animals like bilbies might be a better symbol of Easter. In Australia, chocolate bilbies and bunnies are made in many shapes and sizes.

A bilby

Bilby Facts

Bilbies live in dry, desert areas in Australia, where they dig spiral-shaped burrows for shelter. Bilbies are marsupials, which means they carry their young in a small pouch. They eat plants, insects, spiders and other small animals. A bilby can grow to 50 centimetres in length.

Haigh's Helps an Endangered Species

Since the introduction of rabbits, foxes and cats to Australia, the bilby population has fallen so much the bilby is now endangered. Haigh's Chocolates wanted to help the bilby – so in 1993, they stopped making Easter bunnies. Haigh's started making chocolate Easter bilbies instead.

Chocolate Easter bilbies help remind Australians of their own native animals. Money from every Haigh's bilby sold is donated to organisations that work to save Australia's real bilbies.

Haigh's chocolate bilbies

8 A CHOCOLATE
School

Rebecca at her school

Who wouldn't love to go to a chocolate school? The Sydney Chocolate School in Mosman, Australia, teaches people of all ages how to make chocolates. The teacher, Rebecca, trained to be a *chocolatier** in France, Europe. Nowadays, she really loves teaching children all about making chocolates, such as chocolate frogs, freckles and nests.

Chocolates are made by pouring melted chocolate into moulds.

Other colourful treats or pieces of fruit can be added to the melted chocolate.

Learning how to make chocolates can be messy – but a *lot* of fun!

And, if you're lucky, you might get to pop chocolate-dipped balloons!

* A chocolatier *is the French name for someone who makes and sells chocolates.*